THE WEDDING OF GINGER & BASIL

A COMPANION NOVELLA, A GINGER GOLD MYSTERY

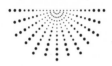

LEE STRAUSS

SUMMARY

PLEASE NOTE: BRITISH SPELLING IS USED IN THIS BOOK.

For fans of Ginger Gold and Basil Reed - this is the wedding you've been waiting for! The bride and groom prepare for their big day and, of course, things don't go exactly as planned. Told from the alternating points of view of many of the beloved characters in the world of Ginger Gold, you'll find yourself holding your breath, anticipating that happily ever after.

The Wedding of Ginger & Basil a companion novella best enjoyed after book 7 (Murder at St. George's Church) in the Ginger Gold Mystery series.

This is a mystery, but not a murder mystery.

GINGER

Ginger Hartigan Gold, soon to be Mrs. Basil Reed, awoke early with the first light of dawn. Once her mind registered the importance of the day, there was no going back to sleep. As if sensing his mistress' restlessness, her black-and-white Boston terrier pressed a damp nose against her cheek.

"Good morning, Bossy," Ginger murmured into the pup's ear as she cradled him.

Now, propped up against fluffy pillows in her bed sipping tea, Ginger picked up the two envelopes that sat unopened on her bedside cabinet: one from her half-sister Louisa, and one from her good friend Haley Higgins. She opened Haley's first.

Dearest Ginger,

Would it be the height of conceit if I said I told you so? I know what you're thinking, "But you didn't even like Basil Reed!" Not so. I liked him well enough though he made me worried about you, especially where it concerned his late wife. You can't fault me for that. However, all's well that ends well. I'm just sorry I can't be there to share the happy occasion with you.

Thank you again for your kind offer to come to Boston to help with the murder investigation of my brother Joe. Whoever the killer is, he—or she, perhaps—is long gone. Unlike England, America isn't an island, and it's enormous with countless places to hide. Best you stay where you are and make Basil a happy man!

I'll be returning to Boston University to finish my medical training. I've been offered a summer position with the city coroner thanks to the glowing referral from Dr. Gupta. Family gatherings are tough without Joe, but as they say, the living must keep on living.

I hope you receive this letter in time. You are always in my thoughts, especially on your wedding day.

Greetings to Felicia and Ambrosia.

Sending my love,

Haley

Ginger smiled as she wiped a tear from her cheek. "Oh, Haley. I do miss you." Boss whimpered from his spot at the foot of the bed. "You miss her too," Ginger said to him. "Don't you?"

Boss uncurled himself, pushed up on his paws, and took a moment to stretch—his stub of a tail pushing upwards. A large yawn followed before he padded to the warmth of Ginger's side and curled up. Ginger laughed at this lackadaisical demonstration and playfully rubbed his ears. "You are so amusing, old boy."

She ripped open the other envelope, sure to be less sentimental than Haley's script.

Dear Ginger,

Now I understand why you didn't want me to get attached to the dashing Chief Inspector Reed. You had your sights on him! Why didn't you tell me you planned to get married? I would've stayed in London for the wedding. Mother won't let me near the docks after my last "rash act of rebellion," so there's no way I can return on such short notice. Besides, the trip home was unpleasant with stormy weather and rocky seas. A tin bucket should not be a girl's fashion accessory, if you know what I mean.

Are you aware that in America, Basil is pronounced BAYsil? Like the herb? Which is an odd sort of name for a man if you think about it. But odd names are typical of the English, aren't they?

Well, at least give everyone my love, especially Felicia. Mother says congratulations.

Sincerely,

Louisa

"My dear sister, you make me smile." Ginger let out a contented breath and scanned her bedroom. This had been her sanctuary as a child, and again for the last two years since she'd returned from Boston. Only once had she not slept in this bed alone, and that was on her honeymoon with Daniel. So long ago—eleven years— yet in some ways, it felt like yesterday.

She'd redecorated recently. Aqua-green walls and plush green-and-white Persian carpets gave it a fresh new look. The ornate wooden furniture—extravagant four-poster bed with matching dressing table and chest of drawers—remained the same. The gold-and-white striped wingback chairs flanking the tall east-facing windows had been replaced by creamy-white pincushion armchairs and the curtains with breezy white netting.

Basil would like it.

Daniel would forgive her.

After laying her teacup and saucer on the bedside cabinet, she opened the top drawer and removed the photo of her soldier.

"I think you and Basil would get on," she said to the image. "He makes me happy. I do hope you approve."

Whether Daniel would approve or not, her season of mourning him must end. She threw back the covers, swung slender legs off the bed, and pushed herself to her feet. Wrapping the framed photo in an old silk negligée, a gift from Daniel, she buried it underneath the other garments in her chest of drawers. For one last moment, she allowed her mind to wander: meeting Daniel, their wedding, and his death. It was time to put it all away. She had Basil now, and she was excited to begin their life journey together.

Ginger pulled on the top drawer of her dressing table and removed the small ring box that held Basil's wedding band. As she opened the box, a harsh dread raced through her. The ring was gone.

PIPPINS

Mr. Clive Pippins allowed himself a low grunt as he lowered himself onto a plain wooden chair. He wore a soft grey suit chosen by Lady Gold herself. Over the seven decades he'd been walking God's green earth, he'd never imagined he'd have an opportunity to wear such a fine suit or be privileged enough to participate in an occasion that would merit it.

A pair of shiny leather shoes came with the outfit and sat tidily on the wooden floor in front of him. Using a handmade shoehorn, he slipped the shoes on and grinned. They felt as comfortable as his slippers.

The servants' quarters were in the attic. Pippins' small room was orderly with a narrow bed, a short chest of drawers, and a table with a water pitcher and bowl. Seated in the lone chair, Pippins could see a partial image of himself in the mirror. His neck jutted forward, and his head was as bald as a baby's. Skin hung from his bony cheekbones in lines and folds. Funny. In his mind, he was a young man, tall with a ruddy complexion. His eyes, still a brilliant cornflower-blue, were now overpowered by the sagging weight of his eyelids.

Pippins smiled. There was no greater joy in life than to have witnessed a precocious little girl blossom into a capable and confident lady. When the redheaded baby came into the world, he'd rejoiced with the family. What a lovely addition to the household! And then, soon afterwards, he shared in the grief when Mrs. Hartigan passed away. Joy and sorrow. Two sides of the same coin.

Little Ginger Hartigan was the only person with whom Pippins had broken protocol. The child had few playmates and was lonely, so Pippins occasionally stepped into that role with games of I Spy and Noughts and Crosses.

He'd grieved silently when, eight years later, Mr. Hartigan took the girl to Boston. Little Ginger could brighten the dreariest day, and her departure left a void in Pippins' heart. Mr. Hartigan had been good enough to recommend Pippins, and he'd stayed employed all those years. It was only when he'd been reinstated at Hartigan House—on Lady Gold's permanent return to London—that a certain skip returned to his step.

Ever aware of the time, Pippins hoisted himself to his feet, a simple exercise that had become increasingly difficult as the years marched on. The stairs were trying. Many narrow and worn steps led from the top of the house to the main floor. With fingers bent and crooked, he gripped the well-used bannister, which was loose in some parts. The trick was to go slowly. Respect the pain in his knees.

He positioned himself in the entrance hall where he stood, hands behind his back, and waited. Apparently, Lady Gold was to be late to her own wedding. That was fine, he thought. It was a lady's prerogative.

The doorbell resounded, surprising the old butler. Deliveries were made to the rear of the house, and the taxicabs coming for staff and family were not yet due to arrive. He opened the door to find a well-dressed gentleman with a mass of dark-brown floppy hair and a grin so large it could, most probably, block the sun.

"Good morning," Pippins said politely.

"Is this the residence of Lady Gold?"

"It is, but she is quite busy, I'm afraid."

"Yes, I'm aware she's being married today. It'll only take a moment of her time, I assure you."

Pippins opened the door and offered entrance. "I'll ask if she'll see you. Your name?"

"Smith. James Smith."

BASIL

Chief Inspector Basil Reed instructed the removal men as they carried the last of his furniture destined for storage at his parents' country home onto the back of the wooden lorry. This reminded him that he needed to pick up the Honourable Harry Reed and Mrs. Elizabeth Reed at the train station in an hour.

With plenty of time and money, his parents travelled to exotic places. Basil received regular letters from them with postage stamps from Africa, India, and Asia. The most recent post came from Thailand. "Paradise," they'd said. Basil worried they mightn't come for the wedding even though the date for the ceremony had been chosen to fit their itinerary.

"Is that all of it, sir?" the lorry driver asked. His voice echoed in the cleared-out foyer of Basil's Mayfair townhouse. Basil took in the stripped-down living room. A void replaced the sofa and armchairs. The side table that housed his spirits was gone, and walls that had displayed his artwork were blank. The stone hearth was empty and cold.

He had suggested that he and Ginger should live as a couple here where they'd have more privacy and quiet than what would be afforded them at Hartigan House. Ginger had said no. She explained that her responsibilities to Ambrosia and Felicia remained, along with her ward, Scout Elliot. And her dear butler, Pippins, who'd been with the family since she was a child.

Ginger had refrained from mentioning the fact that Basil's late wife had lived here, but he read that in her look. Even he admitted to disconcerting recollections that triggered memories of the heartache she'd inflicted on him with her scandalous and unfaithful ways.

"You're ready to go," Basil said to the lorry driver. He handed the fellow an envelope with cash and confirmed the load's destination.

Basil rechecked his watch. He wasn't the kind to get nervous—his job dealing with the criminal element in one of the fastest growing cities in the world exposed him to plenty of unnerving situations—but getting married to the lovely Lady Georgia Gold, his beloved Ginger, had him on pins and needles.

At forty-one years old, Basil often reflected on his life. He'd enlisted in the army in August, 1914. His experience in the Great War had disappointed him. After a mere thirteen months, he was shot in the stomach, lost his spleen, and nearly died. Soon after, he was deemed unfit to fight.

Working for the London Metropolitan Police had been a way to continue to do his bit for the war effort. Though a member of the peerage and not in financial need, Basil had stayed on with Scotland Yard.

A small pit of anxiety formed in his gut when he recalled how he'd almost lost Ginger. Now that she'd agreed to be his wife, he'd never be so foolish again. He'd make sure she always knew he valued and loved her. Though there was a decade between them, he saw her as his equal, both socially and intellectually. They would be a team on every level even though his promise to support her work as a private investigator would be a hard one to keep. His instinct to protect her was strong.

Basil startled at the shrill ring of his telephone. Had he forgotten to cancel the line? He thought it must be Ginger and answered with a note of anticipation. His eagerness snapped to dismay.

"Chief Inspector Reed—"

"Superintendent Morris. What can I do for you?"

"There's a body in Notting Hill."

His voice was like a foghorn, and Basil held the candlestick apparatus away from his ear.

"I need you to begin the inquiry," Morris said.

"But," Basil sputtered, "I'm getting married at noon! What about Jenkins? Can't he take this one?"

"The crazy bloke broke his arm playing cricket. Don't ask me how. He's with the doc right now and shall take over once the cast is on. Everyone else is on a case, including me."

Basil sighed. "Very well. I'm on my way."

Just before Basil opened the driver's door of his forest-green Austin 7, a courier pedalled up.

"Telegram, sir,"

Basil thanked the lad, read the message, and frowned. It was from his parents. They'd missed their ship and, regrettably, would miss the wedding. They sent their love and looked forward to seeing him at Christmas.

Swallowing his disappointment, Basil stepped on the

clutch and pressed the starter button. The Austin's engine knocked ominously before puttering to silence. Basil tried again, but the motorcar refused to start.

"Blimey!" Basil slammed the door getting the tail of his trench coat caught. He disengaged it without tearing the fabric then ran towards the nearest taxicab and waved the driver down.

MRS. BEASLEY

Mrs. Beasley, as round as she was tall, tottered about the kitchen instructing the staff: Grace, the scullery maid; Lizzie, the parlour maid; and young Scout, Ginger's ward, who often helped inside when the outside work was finished. She wouldn't allow the lad to do more than peel potatoes or sweep the floor, but there was always plenty of that to do. Mrs. Beasley was determined to make sure the food for the drawing room party after the wedding was perfect.

"Lizzie!" Mrs. Beasley clapped red, pudgy hands in front of the young maid's face.

The faraway look and the soft smile the girl wore disappeared.

"Focus on what you're doing! It's about to burn!" Mrs. Beasley scolded.

"Yes, Mrs. Beasley." Lizzie's spindly arm stirred the pot of caramel sauce.

Lizzie was Mrs. Beasley's most reliable helper, and when prestigious occasions like this one arose, it was all hands on deck in the kitchen.

"If I had a title and all the ease and pleasures of life that came with it," Grace said to Lizzie, "I'd never give it up for a man, especially if I had my own money to boot."

Mrs. Beasley glanced at Grace as she waited for Lizzie's response. As expected, the girl took a sentimental and romantic view, no doubt from reading those God-awful romance novels Mrs. Beasley disapproved of.

"True love is willing to sacrifice all," Lizzie said, swooning.

Grace scoffed. "That's naivety and foolishness talkin'."

"Tell that to Lady Gold," Lizzie spouted back. "True love can conquer anything. It's only those who never have experienced it who are sceptical."

"You're an expert on love, now are you? Just because Mr. L—"

"You quiet up right now, Grace," Lizzie said sternly. The wave of red that crept up the maid's neck wasn't due entirely to the heat from the stove. One had to be blind not to see that Lizzie was soft on young Arnold Lowery, the greengrocer's boy who delivered fresh garden produce each morning, and Mrs. Beasley suspected Lizzie of sneaking off to see him. Lowery had brought the Bramley apples currently in the pies now baking in the wood-burning range. The kitchen smelled like heaven.

Mrs. Beasley had known the delivery boy, with his always-dirty face and impish grin, since he was a small lad. One of eight children, Arnold had had his backside walloped by old Mr. Lowery on more than one occasion. Mostly just juvenile mischief but Mrs. Beasley still didn't trust him.

Though she had attended many weddings and served at even more, Mrs. Beasley had never been married. Her title of "Mrs." was a courtesy awarded to her because of her senior position as head cook. She'd been too homely and poor to attract a suitor, and in the end, she'd counted that a blessing. In service since she was ten years old, she'd seen plenty of under-parlour maids and such get in the family way and thrown onto the streets. Most of those servant girls who did find husbands ended up worn to shreds with children coming every year or two like clockwork.

Once the hustle and bustle of this day was over, Mrs. Beasley would give Lizzie a good talking-to. She'd grown fond of the girl whose roving eyes would only bring heartache. Servant life was a good life, particularly with a mistress like Lady Gold. Mrs. Beasley was quite satisfied with her station and position in life, and Lizzie would be wise to follow suit.

It felt like just yesterday when Mrs. Beasley's days as a kitchen maid had started before the break of dawn and didn't end until long after dark. She'd blackened stoves, scrubbed vegetables, polished boots, and ironed bootlaces. She'd worked her way up the kitchen ranks, got small increases in pay, a better bedroom—one with heat—and a softer bed with a quilt that still had a bit of stuffing. It was her dream of becoming a head cook in a respectable house that had kept her going through those hard years. Now, here she was.

She'd be doing a disservice to this younger lot by being too easy on them.

"Grace! The dishes in the scullery shan't wash themselves! Scout, don't miss the dirt in the corners!"

Feeling flushed, Mrs. Beasley balanced herself on

the lone kitchen stool and lifted her swollen feet. Life as she knew it was about to change; it always did when someone new took up residence in the house, and this gentleman was enlisting for a long time. It wasn't like there weren't any men about Hartigan House. There was Clement, the gardener, and Pippins, but they were servants, where Mr. Reed would be master. What sort of requirements would he bring?

Lady Gold was happy, and that was all Mrs. Beasley cared about now. After today, she'd simply be Mrs. Reed. She must love this Chief Inspector to accept a society drop such as that. But Mrs. Beasley wasn't about to judge.

An acrid scent irritated her nostrils. She jumped to her feet, waddled like a running duck to the stove, and opened the oven door. Smoke streamed to the ceilings.

"Lizzie!"

Grabbing a potholder, Mrs. Beasley deftly removed the steaming hot Bramley apple pies. "Dear Lord!"

"Only one's been burned," Grace said as she peered around Mrs. Beasley's stout body. "And not badly."

Mrs. Beasley had the nose of a hound when it came to her baked goods. Grace was correct, a revelation that surprised the cook. She'd assumed Grace's lowly demeanour reflected mental slowness. Could it be she'd misjudged the girl?

"It's not as if we have time to make another one," Mrs. Beasley said. "It shall have to do."

"There're the biscuits that Lizzie and I baked, as well," Grace offered.

Mrs. Beasley narrowed small dark eyes and scanned the kitchen. "Where *is* Lizzie?"

Scout was there, standing still as a tombstone, taking in the drama.

"Scout, did Lizzie say where she was going? Did the mistress ring for her?" Mrs. Beasley didn't like to admit it, but her hearing wasn't what it used to be. "Speak up, boy!"

Scout stammered, "I-I dun't know where Lizzie's gone to, and the missus din't ring."

Mrs. Beasley wiped the moisture that dotted her wrinkled forehead with the edge of her apron. "Grace, go and fetch her, will you? We've still got a lot of work to do."

FELICIA

Felicia Gold had been wearing her wedding finery for an hour already, long before breakfast, which was so unlike her. She'd dressed in a soft pink chiffon frock under a metallic lace coat. She paired this with an ostrich-feather boa and a tight-fitting turban hat, which shrouded the short dark hair that framed her youthful, teardrop face splendidly. On her feet were matching satin-silk shoes with large sparkly clasps. Felicia knew the outfit was flamboyant for the occasion but didn't care. The largesse was a necessity: it helped to conceal her sadness.

She wished she hadn't been so quick to apply her makeup—a lighter and softer touch than when she went dancing at the clubs—for fear of messing her mascara with tears. She must not give in to this barrel of emotion that threatened to burst like a new well.

It wasn't as if Ginger's marriage to Basil Reed would change anything . . . would it? Ginger had reassured her that she and her grandmother could stay at Hartigan House for as long as they liked. They'd just have to get accustomed to a man about the house. Even though she and Ambrosia had only lived there a year, London felt like home. Country living at Bray Manor was a distant memory.

Felicia started at the light knock on her bedroom door, and when she called out, she was stunned to see Ginger wearing a housedress.

"Ginger? I thought you were Lizzie coming to tell me the taxicab had arrived. Why are you not dressed? Oh, goodness, I should have offered to help!" Her shoulders collapsed into herself after that outburst. "Of course, you have Lizzie for that." Felicia's expression crumpled, and she jumped from her chair. She extracted a handkerchief from her bedside cabinet and sobbed into it.

Alarmed, Ginger hurried to her side. "What's the matter, love? Has something happened?"

Felicia blinked with watery eyes. "No, nothing terrible. This is a *very* happy day. I'm simply *happy* for you!"

Ginger drew her sister-in-law into a gentle embrace. "Is this about Daniel?"

Felicia's body shook as she fought back the tears. "I'm worried he is being forgotten."

Felicia had lost her parents to a carriage accident when she was too young to remember. Daniel had been old enough to make his own way, but Felicia had fallen into the care of her bereft and overbearing grandmother, the Dowager Lady Ambrosia Gold.

"I'll never forget Daniel," Ginger said kindly. "I loved him. A part of my heart shall always belong to him."

Felicia dabbed at her reddening nose. "I rarely mention him, but that doesn't mean I don't think of him every day."

"You can speak of him to me at any time," Ginger said. "I'd welcome it."

"But, you'll be married to another man. Wouldn't that be strange? Oh, Lord." Felicia's brow furrowed. "Shall we still be sisters-in-law?"

"We shall always be sisters," Ginger said. "No matter what the law says."

Felicia relaxed in Ginger's arms. "You're too good to me." She gently pulled away and ran the tip of her handkerchief under her eyes. "I've ruined my makeup."

"You look beautiful, Felicia."

"At least I have my gown on. Now allow me to assist you with yours. It'll never do to be late to the church. Poor Basil might think you've left him at the altar."

"There is something I could use your help with," Ginger said.

"What is it?"

"I seem to have misplaced Basil's ring."

AMBROSIA

Dowager Lady Ambrosia Gold sat in the quiet of the little-used drawing room. She found the contrasting pastel colours of the furniture and wallpaper satisfying. Rose-coloured netting on the large windows brightened the area with a warm glow. It had a sophistication that the sitting room, where the younger set gathered, somehow had missed. Here she could think without the ridiculous hullabaloo that permeated the rest of Hartigan House at any given time.

Captivated by the flames snapping in the hearth, she let her mind wander back to her own wedding day, so many years ago. The world was a different place then. Ladies were satisfied with their station in the home: managing servants, bringing up children, supporting good causes. How she missed her days running Bray Manor in Chesterton.

The female persuasion knew about decorum and polite society. Her own beloved granddaughter continued to be a source of dismay and embarrassment in that regard. Not only were the girl's antics unsuitable for one of her station, but her wardrobe choice often caused the Dowager Lady Gold to nearly faint. What would be next? Young ladies baring their knees?!

Ambrosia had had a privileged upbringing, and her 1870 marriage to Sir Artemis Gold had guaranteed a comfortable lifestyle amongst the elite. Her lips tugged up into a small smile as she recalled her handsome groom. He'd pursued her openly, as a gentleman should. Their engagement had been short and their wedding large. She'd been so young and naive then, only eighteen. Had she known the heartache ahead of her, she might've committed herself to spinsterhood.

The muscles in her face relaxed back into a frown. The lines etched around her shrinking eyes and thinning lips told the story of many hard years. There was the lost child. No one knew about the untimely delivery because one didn't discuss personal matters such as that. Blessedly, the next one, a son, had lived.

Alas, there were to be no more children. Despite this, Ambrosia had been quite happy for a long while, not knowing her dear husband had got himself entangled with the sin of gambling. It wasn't until Ambrosia's son Jonathon had married—and what a sum was spent on the event!—did she suspect. When Artemis unexpectedly died of a heart attack, the devastating truth of the matter came to light. They were destitute.

Somehow, with Jonathon's help, they managed to keep Bray Manor, and more importantly, keep up appearances. Then another unbearable tragedy struck. Both Jonathon and his wife were killed in a carriage mishap.

Then Daniel announced he was going to America to marry Georgia Hartigan and save the family from financial ruin. Arranged marriages had stood the test of time and tradition. It was pure luck, or perhaps, the grace of God that Daniel and Ginger had actually fallen in love.

A tap on the drawing-room door was followed by the entrance of Ambrosia's maid, Langley, a tall, thin woman with arms as long as an ape's.

"Set the tray there," Ambrosia instructed.

"Can I get you anything else, madam?"

"Nothing, thank you. You may leave."

Ambrosia's long, gnarled fingers stroked her grey, shingled bob. It had grown out since her foolish and impulsive salon trip that had resulted in this vanity, but growing it out meant a pile of hairpins poking into her scalp. She simply couldn't tolerate the discomfort. When one had as many years behind her as she had, one had to grasp for comfort wherever one could. She had gradually become used to her new look when she studied her reflection in the mirror, but she did miss the weight of her bun on her head. It made her feel as if she was donning a crown or a tiara, especially once decorated with gem-encrusted clips and pins.

She sipped the hot morning tea, ignoring the tremor in her hands. Ageing was for the birds!

A large framed portrait of Ginger's parents, when they were young and both alive, hung prominently on the wall. The former master and mistress of Hartigan House would soon be officially replaced by the next generation. Ambrosia was happy with the match. Basil —she called him by his Christian name now that he was to be family—was from fine stock. Though, for some unfathomable reason, he remained in public service. His father was an Honourable and the title would one day land on Basil Reed. And if she were honest, she was happy not to share the title, Lady Gold. Ginger, bless her heart, was a commoner by blood, though no one would have guessed it had they not already known. Ambrosia secretly disliked that Ginger had a title when her own granddaughter, her own flesh and blood, had none.

Though her hearing was going, the Dowager Lady Gold could still make out a commotion in the hall. She rang for her maid.

"My lady," the maid said with a slight bending of the knees.

"Langley, what on earth is going on now? Shouldn't everyone be leaving soon for the church?"

"Yes, madam. But there seems to be a bit of trouble. Lady Gold's ring is missing."

"Missing? Which ring?"

"The wedding ring, madam. The one she means to give to the chief inspector."

GINGER

Ginger began a frantic search for Basil's ring starting with her chest of drawers. Piece by piece, she flung her silk and satin lingerie on the bed. "I might have placed it here when my mind was elsewhere."

"You have had a lot on your plate lately," Felicia said as she opened the drawers of the closest bedside cabinet.

After a thorough search of each drawer, Ginger checked every hatbox and the pockets of every frock hanging in her wardrobe. "It has to be somewhere! The wedding is in one hour! How could I have misplaced Basil's ring!"

She fell to her hands and knees to search under her furnishings.

Felicia stared at her with dismay. "Ginger!"

"I might have dropped it." Ginger's growing desperation drove her to look in even the most ridiculous places, including under the rug and inside her shoes.

"Life's become quite chaotic since my engagement," she said stripping the sheets off the bed. The bed clothes fluttered like sails shimmering in a mighty wind.

Felicia nodded sheepishly. "I should have been more help to you."

Ginger waved off Felicia's belated concern. It was true that Ginger had been busier than usual with the running of her dress shop, Feathers & Flair—autumn was a trying season for fashion—along with managing her household of staff at Hartigan House. She could have hired an assistant if she needed help. Apparently, she was too busy to see she had indeed needed help. Oh, mercy.

And she mustn't forget about her young ward, Scout Elliot. Where was he anyway? Ginger always made a point of spending time with him each morning but had failed in that regard lately. Today, she hadn't even set eyes on the wiry lad. The fact that Boss had also disappeared reassured Ginger that the two were likely together.

"Perhaps Lizzie or Grace moved it somewhere safe when they cleaned your room," Felicia said.

Ginger simply hummed. She appreciated Felicia's attempt to soothe her, but they both knew that neither maid would dare to touch such an item of value, much less move it.

Ginger and Felicia stared at the ransacked mess. "It's not here," Ginger whispered. She glanced at her watch again. Time was ticking!

"I need to inquire of the staff," Ginger said. "Someone in this house must know where the ring is."

Ginger gripped the wooden bannister of the elegant staircase that curved down from the second level to the ground floor entrance. Her slippered feet padded against the plush red runner as her silk nightdress floated behind her. Pippins waited on the black and white tiles, standing as straight as a septuagenarian might, with his white-gloved hands folded. He looked quite handsome in the suit she'd ordered for him.

Reading her look of consternation, the butler asked, "Is something the matter, madam?"

"Yes. I can't seem to find Basil's ring."

Pippins' grey bushy brows subtly raised. "Madam?"

"The one I'm meant to give to Basil at the ceremony." A nervous check of her watch told her only two minutes had passed since the last time she looked.

"I see. What would you like me to do?"

"Please assemble the staff in the sitting room."

Pippins bowed and pivoted toward the back of the house.

Felicia, who'd escorted Ginger down the stairs, said, "Do you think someone's *stolen* it?"

"No, at least I hope not. But I need everyone's help to locate it. I can't show up at the church without it!"

Pippins was the first to return to the sitting room, followed by Clement the gardener, and Grace. Ginger sat in her favourite armchair facing the fireplace and stared at the Waterhouse masterpiece, *The Mermaid*, returned to its position above the mantel. The redheaded beauty reminded Ginger of her mother whose red locks Ginger had inherited. The artwork brought her comfort, but today she wished she could reach into the painting and draw Basil's ring from the jewels within.

"Where is everyone else?" she asked.

"Mrs. Beasley needs a couple of minutes in the kitchen, madam," Grace said. The maid sat board-straight with wide eyes darting around the room.

"I'll round up the others," Felicia offered and left by the dining room door.

"I'll start with those present," Ginger said. "Dear Pips, I gather you've seen or heard nothing about a gold wedding band distributed somewhere in the house, or possibly, outside in the grounds?"

"No, madam. I would've mentioned it immediately had I witnessed such an item out of place."

"Of course. I'm asking only as a matter of form."

Ginger called on Clement. "You've little reason to be indoors, but perhaps I've accidentally dropped the ring outside after driving the Crossley. Would you mind taking a gander? Both inside the motorcar and the garage, and the pathway to the house."

Clement jumped to his feet. "I shall be most thorough in my search, madam."

"Thank you."

Grace Duncan stared at her hands. The poor thing wasn't accustomed to being alone in a room with her mistress. Ginger spoke gently, "Grace, when was the last time you worked on the second floor?"

"Just this morning, madam. I dusted and hoovered the spare rooms and the hallways."

Ginger remembered hearing the vacuum cleaner motor. "Can you tell me the last time you cleaned my bedroom?"

"Just yesterday, madam, but I didn't take anything, I promise. I never take anything that's not mine."

"Of course. Where is Lizzie?"

Grace's chin darted up, and her jaw grew slack. "She's not here, madam?"

"Oh? Where has she gone?"

Grace swallowed. "I really couldn't say."

Ginger inclined her head and studied the young woman. She was lying, and Ginger wanted to know why.

"You don't need to protect her. I'm sure whatever she's up to, she means well."

"I'm certain of that as well, madam."

Before Ginger could say more, the sitting room door flew open and Ambrosia entered, her walking stick tapping the wood floors with authority. Ginger excused Grace with instructions to relieve Mrs. Beasley.

Ambrosia reclined in a sturdy pincushion chair. Her maid, Langley, sweeping behind her.

"What's this about a missing ring?"

"The ring I bought for Basil—his wedding ring—is gone."

"Gone?"

"Well, I can't find it. I'm certain I left it in its box in my dressing table drawer, but it's possible I misplaced it."

"One does not misplace valuable jewellery."

"Langley," Ginger started, "you haven't come across it, have you?"

A startled expression overcame the maid's long face. "I have not." She scowled at the implication. "I certainly would never steal anything."

"Of course not," Ambrosia blustered. "That's preposterous." She glowered at Ginger for even suggesting such a thing. "A stranger must have done it. Hartigan House isn't exactly secure. Doors and windows are left unlocked all the time. You must face the facts, Ginger. You've been robbed."

Pippins cleared his throat.

"Yes?" Ginger prompted.

"There was that gentleman who called earlier."

"Oh, yes, I remember. I was in no position to take a caller, especially a stranger. What was his name again?"

"Mr. James Smith."

Ambrosia huffed. "An alias if there ever was one. There's your thief, Ginger. Mark my words."

Ginger groaned. What was she supposed to do now? Ring Basil to report that his wedding band had been stolen? And how was she to reach him? He certainly wouldn't be at Scotland Yard—he was locking up his townhouse in Mayfair. She'd had his wedding suit sent to Brown's Hotel where he was staying.

Mrs. Beasley waddled into the room all hot and flustered, wiping her damp brow dramatically. "My lady, shouldn't we all be dressing for the wedding?"

"Yes, indeed we should, Mrs. Beasley," Ginger said. "However, you may have heard that the gold wedding ring intended for Chief Inspector Reed has disappeared."

Mrs. Beasley actually paled. "Oh, no, I hadn't, madam."

"Is there something to report, Mrs. Beasley? You seem unsettled."

"Well, it's just young Lizzie, madam. She's been making eyes at the greengrocer's lad. I believe they're sweet on each other. I think they might have . . ."

Ginger's stomach sank. "Eloped?"

"Yes, madam. Young girls lose their heads sometimes when they believe they've fallen in love. You don't think she took . . . It costs money to elope. One might check the trains to Gretna Green."

"There's no evidence to support such an assumption as yet," Ginger said. Her heart was troubled. She liked

Lizzie. Trusted her to care for Boss and Scout. Trusted her with her expensive wardrobe and personal things. She'd never dreamed that Lizzie could be capable of something so devious. If she felt she had to steal to pay for her elopement why take the wedding band? Ginger had plenty of nice jewellery worth more money. It just didn't make sense.

The only one left to talk to was her ward, Scout. Grace was being tight-lipped, but Ginger knew that people often ignored the children in their midst when they conversed. Perhaps he'd heard something that would reveal where Lizzie had gone. Ginger checked her wristwatch and flew to her feet. She was most certainly going to be late to her wedding.

"Mrs. Beasley, would you happen to know where Scout is?"

"I told him to get up to the attic and wash, but he scampered outside instead." She shook her head in frustration. "The lad never listens to me unless you specifically tell him to do so."

"I'll find him and insist he apologise," Ginger said.

Before she could make her way to the garden, Pippins demanded her attention.

"Madam, Scotland Yard on the telephone for you."

BASIL

The part Basil disliked the most about his job was witnessing the injustice, the dark side of humanity, or lack of it in some cases. The bloke lying along the stone wall had fallen on hard times, evidenced by the tattered jacket and worn-out boots. His wardrobe, however, was the least of the man's worries. The bloody crevice on the back of his skull had made every worldly problem void.

"Poor rotter," Sergeant Scott said. "Shall I begin taking photographs?"

Basil held his trilby hat against a sudden gust of wind and nodded. To the constable on duty, he asked, "Identity?"

"Nothing on him, sir. I've a man canvassing the area, but so far, no one knows about him. Or, if they do, they're not talking."

"Who discovered the victim?"

"The greengrocer's lad, over there. On his delivery route. Was good enough to use the neighbour's telephone to call it in."

Basil stared in the direction the constable pointed. A

young man in a short jacket and a newsboy cap stood beside a horse and cart, the latter half-full of produce. A worried look glazed his eyes. Sitting in the cart was a young woman, simply dressed in a dark coat with a black cloche on her head. Short strands of mousy-brown hair floated around a pixie-like face pinched with anxiety. She looked vaguely familiar. Her eyes darted to the bunch of flowers she held in gloved hands when she caught him staring. He strolled towards the couple and produced his Met card.

"Chief Inspector Basil Reed. May I have a few words?"

The greengrocer stepped forward and, as if he meant to shield her from the police, he placed his body between Basil and the girl.

"I understand you found the victim," Basil said as he removed a small notebook and pencil from his trench coat pocket.

The greengrocer fidgeted. "Yes, sir, I did."

"Your name?"

"Arnold Lowery."

"I take it you were on your way to make a delivery?"

"Yes, sir. I have several stops on this route. I'm quite behind schedule, and Mrs. Nelson shall be furious. She's bound to report me."

"Death can be an inconvenience," Basil said dryly, feeling the pressure of time himself. He glanced at his watch. An hour and forty-five minutes before he had to be at the church, and he still had to put on his wedding suit. Drat that Jenkins! Where was he? Basil no longer had sympathy for his bloody broken arm.

"When was it that you spotted the man?"

"I'm due at Mrs. Nelson's by eight." Lowery made a

show of checking his wristwatch. I found him about ten minutes before that.

Basil took a small step sideways to view the girl.

"A passenger?" he asked Lowery. "A job on the side as a taxi driver, perhaps?"

"She's a friend. I offered her a lift to save her from walking in poor weather."

"Very gentlemanly of you." And a convenient alibi. "I'd like a word with her."

"She's nothing to do with it, sir. In the cart the whole time."

"She's a witness," Basil explained. "Such as it is."

Lowery sighed and reluctantly stepped aside. The look on the young lady's face was dreadful. Basil doubted it was due to the hard wooden seat of the cart.

"Miss . . . ?" Basil prompted.

"Miss Weaver, sir."

"Christian name?"

Miss Weaver hesitated. "Elizabeth."

Basil was sure he'd seen this face before. Plain, with no paint or powder, simple clothing. In service, he guessed. "Where are you headed today, Miss Weaver?"

The girl swallowed, her focus jumped to the green-grocer and back to the flowers in her hands. "Just errands to run, sir."

Had the couple been about to elope? It was a common enough event. Weddings were expensive, too much so for many in the lower classes. If this was the case, it was decent of Mr. Lowery to take time to call in the violent death of the nameless victim.

He was about to let them go when recognition dawned. The girl was one of Ginger's maids!

"Miss Weaver, one would assume that your mistress could be in need of your assistance today."

The young maid's lower lip trembled. "Yes sir. I'm dreadfully sorry, sir. What can be done, sir?"

"Please wait here for a moment," he said to both Miss Weaver and Mr. Lowery.

Sergeant Scott had completed his photography and was packing his Furet camera and blown flashbulbs away. Two constables stood beside him.

"Murder weapon?" Basil asked.

A constable held up a large round stone in the palm of a gloved hand. "We found this on the side of the road about half a mile up."

Basil squinted in the dim light of the gloomy day. One side of the stone was marked with a reddish-brown stain. Blood. A more inexperienced eye could have mistaken it for dirt.

"Who found it?" Basil asked.

"I did, sir."

"Well, done, Constable."

The constable blushed. "Thank you, sir."

"Put it in an evidence bag. Perhaps we can pull a fingerprint."

The constable, buoyed with a new burst of confidence, sprinted away to follow his orders.

The medical examiner arrived, and Basil watched as he poked at the victim. The physician groaned as he pressed on the thighs of his trousers and stretched back to a standing position. "Means of death, a conk on the head with a heavy blunt instrument. I presume you've come to that conclusion yourself, Chief Inspector."

"Indeed." Basil sighed. Only one in ten murders in the city of London was solved, and even fewer produced a conviction. The chances of this one reaching the courts were slim to none. Basil could only hope that they discovered the poor man's identity so he could have a proper, dignified burial.

"Shall I have my men take the body to the mortuary?" the medical examiner asked.

Basil shook his head. "No. We must wait for the inspector who shall lead this case. I'm just filling in until he gets here."

"That's highly unusual."

"I'm to be married in less than two hours." Basil's pulse jumped at the urgency. After everything he'd gone through to get Ginger to marry him, he daren't be late! If Jenkins didn't arrive soon, Basil was ready to break his other arm.

Finally, a black taxicab pulled into the alley and came to a stop in front of Basil and Sergeant Scott. An apologetic Inspector Jenkins shifted awkwardly to his feet, his left arm bandaged to his chest.

"Chief Inspector. So sorry to get you messed up in this and on your wedding day, to boot."

Basil wasted no time with pleasantries. He flipped open his notebook and tore out a page. "Here are my notes. You can confirm the details yourself." He nodded to the greengrocer and Ginger's maid—both waiting with distressed looks on their faces as a constable blocked their cart.

"The young man is Arnold Lowery. He found the victim whilst on his morning deliveries. The young lady is Elizabeth Weaver, also called Lizzie, and is in service to my fiancée."

Jenkins raised a brow. "One would think she'd be busy at the house with a bride and a wedding and so forth."

"Indeed. All the same, they're your only witnesses. Perhaps further questioning might jar their memories. It's possible they saw something that they're not currently registering as important."

"Nice bunch of flowers," Jenkins said, staring past Basil's shoulder. "I hope we're not delaying a romantic assignation."

Basil snorted. "As a matter of fact, you are."

"Right, forgive me," Jenkins sputtered. "Get going!"

"Jenkins, do ask someone to ring Lady Gold at Hartigan House."

Basil slapped his pockets looking for his keys then groaned as he remembered how his Austin had failed him.

"I've got a motorcar." Scott stepped in beside Basil and nodded towards the black, hardtop Arrol-Johnston Metropolitan Police vehicle. "Where to?"

"My hotel. I can catch a taxi from there."

Basil lifted the sleeve of his trench coat to check the time. He'd lost an hour. It was tight, but if he dressed quickly and had the good fortune of hailing a cabbie who knew the shortcuts, he'd get to the church on time.

"My missus says, it's bad luck to investigate a murder on a fella's wedding day," Scott announced as he pressed the starter button.

Basil tensed. "One event is in no way connected to the other."

"Right you are," Scott added quickly. "My missus is the superstitious sort. It's all poppycock if ya ask me." He pulled into busy traffic on Bayswater Road.

"Would it be faster to cut the corner through Hyde Park?"

"You might be right about that, sir."

Sergeant Scott took the necessary sharp right onto West Carriage Drive. Two seconds later, the steering wheel tugged out of his hands.

"Whoa!"

Basil grabbed onto the hand strap with one hand and his hat with the other as the motorcar jerked into the ditch.

Scott shrugged helplessly. "I think a tyre blew, sir."

"Blimey!" Basil pushed his weight out of the passenger door. A cursory examination of the mangled tyre was enough to confirm that the police vehicle would get them nowhere fast. He waved at his companion as he jogged back to Bayswater Road. "Help me find a taxicab, man!"

LIZZIE

Lizzie Weaver, nineteen years of age, had been in service since she was twelve. The third of ten children, Lizzie had been dropped off without celebration at the Knight residence, a sprawling manor on the outskirts of London. She would see her parents and younger siblings once a week on Sunday afternoons, her only time off, where she was reminded how impoverished her family was, and how blessed her cold attic room at the manor was in comparison. At least she never went to bed hungry, and her sheets were clean and free of lice.

Through a string of serendipitous events, Mr. Pippins had employed her to help prepare Hartigan House for Lady Gold's return from Boston, and Lizzie had jumped ranks miraculously to the position of a lady's maid. To be sure, she still had to labour in the kitchen when a special occasion demanded it, but at least she was no longer a scullery maid. That drudgery belonged to Grace Duncan. Though Lizzie was younger than Grace—and slighter in stature, not that that was relevant—Lizzie had the good fortune of having seniority, which was a significant distinction in life below stairs. It was because of this status she could extract herself from the heat, both from the kitchen and Mrs. Beasley's mood, for more palatable tasks, such as helping Lady Gold dress.

Now, she had jeopardised it all! Good intentions be damned, even the gracious Lady Gold must have her limits.

The weight of humiliation and despair crushed her soul as she travelled by police motorcar down the back alley and into the rear yard of Hartigan House. Surely, she would be sacked and sent off without a reference! What would she do now? Her family depended on her earnings. Tears welled up behind her eyes as she thought of the disappointment they would experience when they heard.

Mrs. Beasley pulled her roughly into the kitchen. "You stupid, stupid girl! Lady Gold is waiting for you in the sitting room." She pushed Lizzie along through the kitchen, nearly causing her to stumble. "Hurry up. She's about to be wed, and she's not even dressed, all for waiting on the likes of you!"

Lizzie kept her gaze to the floor as she entered the sitting room, the bouquet hanging limply from one dangling arm.

"Lady Gold, I'm so dreadfully sorry."

Like a rose reaching for the sun, Lady Gold stood. "Did you mean to elope with Mr. Lowery on my wedding day?"

Startled by the question, Lizzie's small pointed chin jutted up. "What? No! Madam, of course not."

"The constable from Scotland Yard said you were with Mr. Lowery, and that you appeared to be running off." Lady Gold stared at the drooping bouquet.

Lizzie felt her face flush with mortification. "No, madam, it's not what it looks like."

"Why did you leave Hartigan House today? Mrs. Beasley assures me she hadn't given you permission."

"Oh, Lady Gold. I only meant to be gone for twenty minutes." She lifted the flowers. "As a wedding gift. I know they're your favourite."

Lady Gold's gaze moved to the bunch of pale yellow blossoms, her green eyes flashing with recognition. "Chrysanthemums?"

Lizzie's eyes filled with fresh tears. "I wanted to give you something special, and Mr. Lowery offered to take me on part of his delivery round. He drives right past the hothouse, you see."

"Why didn't you ask Mrs. Beasley?"

"Because Mrs. Beasley can be quite obstinate when she wants. She wouldn't have let me go, and this morning was the only time I could get them fresh."

"Lizzie, have you seen the gold wedding band I purchased for Mr. Reed?"

Lizzie blinked glassy eyes in confusion. "No? Why? Is it missing?" Before Ginger could reply, Lizzie came to her own conclusion and wailed. "I didn't take it, I swear!"

Lizzie had promised herself she'd remain in control of her emotions, take her punishment with dignity. But to be accused of thievery? Her chest heaved, and her shoulders trembled. She erupted into a loud, undignified sob. Thank goodness for Lady Gold's handkerchief!

"Now, now," Lady Gold murmured. "Obviously, it's all been a big misunderstanding. Please, pull yourself together. I'm still not dressed, and I need your help. It shan't do for you to be sniffling over me."

Lizzie couldn't believe her ears. She wasn't being sacked? "Oh, milady, you're so kind. Pure goodness itself! I promise never to disappoint you in such a way again. I'll be the best maid in London until the day I die. I promise!" She hiccupped and quickly put a palm over her mouth.

Her good lady's lips twitched in a smile. "You can start by cleaning up and meeting me in my room."

Lizzie curtsied. "I certainly will, madam, to be sure. I'll be with you in a jiffy."

"Before you go," Ginger said, "would you know where Scout might be? Normally, he's in the thick of things, but today he's quite invisible."

"Oh, my guess is he's in the stable with Goldmine. The horse brings him comfort, that and Boss, as well. He's been out of sorts with your wedding coming up, madam."

Ginger inclined her head. "Oh?"

"He's afraid you shan't have time for him once there's a man in the house. He says he already feels like you're too busy for him." Lizzie froze. Had she said that aloud? Why couldn't she keep her big mouth shut? Especially after being forgiven such an immense blunder. "Please, forgive me, madam. I don't mean to speak out of turn. It's not my business."

Lizzie started for the door when Lady Gold called for her again. "Lizzie?"

"Yes, madam?"

"Get a vase for the chrysanthemums and place them in my room."

Lizzie had nearly forgotten about the tired-looking bouquet. "Yes, madam. I'll do that right away.

SCOUT

Eleven-year-old Scout Elliot had done something bad. For a while, he'd thought he'd got away with it, thought his idea was a good one, and that he'd get what he wanted. Now, he understood that all it would get him was a stint in prison.

He shouldn't be so surprised; crime ran in his family. Perhaps he would see Cousin Marvin again . . . if they were lucky enough to be in the same prison.

"I'm gonna miss you, Goldmine," he said as he brushed the flanks of the exceptionally beautiful creature—an Akhal-Teke, with hair as fine and golden as an angel's.

Of all his chores, Scout loved the stable work the best. The smell of fresh grain, even the scent of horse sweat and dung. Carrying water to fill Goldmine's trough, forking hay for him to eat, shovelling the manure —he loved it all.

Recently, Scout had asked Mr. Clement a very important question. "Do you fink I could grow up to be a jockey?"

Mr. Clement's gaze had moved from the top of Scout's newsboy cap to the toes of his scuffed-up boots. "You're small enough in stature," he'd said.

The one thing Scout had rued mightily was how slight and short he was for his age. He thought that maybe being small was one of those rotten bits of life that could turn into something good. "Right, I am," he'd replied with a new note of pride in his voice. "I just need to learn to ride fast."

Mr. Clement's leathery face had cracked into a smile. "I've no doubt you shall succeed at that if you work hard for it."

"I shall, sir! I shall!"

Scout's lip quivered at the memory as he fought the tears that burned the back of his eyes. He'd no longer get to be a jockey. Not after what he'd done.

A sour swallow scorched Scout's throat. He drew a smooth flannel sleeve under his nose.

Yup, he was no better than Marvin. Scout had been so cross with his cousin when he fell in with those bad folk and got taken away. Their ol' uncle had died, and Marvin was supposed to take care of him. But Marvin had been stupid, and Scout was left alone to fend for himself.

Until the missus came and took him to Hartigan House. Gave him a bed, and food, and dumb schooling, but most of all she made him feel safe. No bad guys would come and slit his throat during the night.

Now, *he* was the bad guy.

"I'm so sorry, missus," he muttered.

He should've left the stable by now, but the thought of going out on his own was paralysing. First, where should he go? Back to east London? Second, how was he to get there? He couldn't afford a taxicab and didn't know how to take the bus or tube. It was too far to walk, and he was bound to get lost if he tried.

Scout patted Goldmine's long nose as the large animal's great streamer of a tail swished back and forth to swat at flies. Scout held out a flattened palm with a treat. A bright red, autumn apple.

"Your favourite, ol' boy."

An evil idea passed through his mind. He could take Goldmine to get away. Not for good, just to get *somewhere else*, then he'd tell the horse to go home. Horses were clever that way.

Except, it would hurt the missus if he did that, and he'd harmed her enough already. Especially on this *very important* day.

Scout mused on the concept of marriage as he tackled Goldmine's left flank. He knew that gentlemen and ladies got married in a church, and then the babies would come. His small mouth pulled down in a deeper frown, seemingly moving the freckles on his nose forward. Would the missus get a new baby? Scout felt a strange unpleasant sensation burn in his chest. It wasn't like he was the missus' own son, but she treated him well, and she was the closest thing to a mother he'd ever had. It was something the missus and himself had in common—they'd both lost their mothers before they could remember them.

The missus was so busy that she never had time to see him anymore, anyway. All because of *him*. A knot of bitterness tightened in his chest. With a new master around, Scout would be invisible. He could leave and not be missed.

Before he did, he would return what he'd taken. It

was the right thing to do. But how? Now that the house was such a bustle of activity, someone was sure to see him. If he were caught, he'd be gaoled for sure!

He reached up, wrapped his thin, bony arms around the gelding's muscular neck, and dampened his white-gold mane with his tears.

The words stuck in his throat and took a great effort to get out. "G-goodbye, G-goldmine."

"Scout?"

Scout jumped backwards, nearly tripping on a pitch-fork. His eyes widened with fear at the silhouette in the barn door.

"Missus?" he mustered. Lady Gold's features brightened as she stepped towards him. The afternoon light had broken through the clouds and cascaded against her soft skin. Her red hair, wavy around her ears, shone like a bright crimson sun. She wore a purple, oriental house-dress that fluttered in the crisp autumn breeze. Her cheeks were blushing, and her breath was as quick as if she'd run to find him. Scout could barely breathe. The missus was the most lovely lady he'd ever seen.

"Dear, dear Scout," Lady Gold said. Her words were silky and sounded kind.

Scout would miss her *so much*.

"Yes, missus?" His voice was timid, like a squeaky mouse.

Lady Gold lowered herself to one knee, not even caring about the hay and dust on the stable floor. Her green eyes, so green they sparkled like dew-covered moss, were sad and caring. "Is there something you need to tell me?"

OLIVER

Reverend Oliver Hill adjusted his stiff, white dog collar as he readied himself in front of the mirror. He looked forward to the ceremony he was to officiate. His good friend, Lady Ginger Gold, was soon to be married, and Oliver couldn't be happier for her.

He squirted oil into his palms, rubbed them together, and ducked for a better look at his reflection. He smoothed the oil into his hair. A shorter vicar had once lived in the parsonage before Oliver, and now for Matilda's sake, Oliver had had to learn to live with the mirror placement. He'd spent his whole life making adjustments for his long legs, and so this minor inconvenience was nothing new.

He and his wife Matilda—*his wife*—he still wasn't used to saying those words. The three months he'd been married had been the most delightful three months of his life. How blessed he was to have found such a brilliant lady to share the rest of his life. And now, Ginger should enjoy this holiest of unions as well.

Oliver remembered their first meeting. Ginger had

wandered into St. George's Church and claimed a pew near the back. Oliver spotted her in the nave from his view at his desk in the vestry. He'd learned to give seekers of peace a little time before approaching and offering counsel. Ginger had been reticent, people of her station in life usually were, but Oliver managed to make her comfortable with polite conversation. Gradually, she'd confided that she had become attracted to a man, the first since her dear husband's death several years earlier, and she couldn't help but feel torn. Guilty, even.

He'd asked her questions about her husband, Lord Daniel Gold, and Ginger's countenance had brightened. She loved to talk about him, and that in the end was the problem. If she allowed another man into her life, into *that* place in her life, would she forget Daniel?

"There are many kinds of love," Oliver had said. "And sometimes, the way the love is expressed must change. For instance, a mother loves her infant in a different manner than she does when the child is grown and gone. The love you feel for Daniel has changed, must change, but you can still love him. If you're unable to talk about him with this new fellow, perhaps there are others in your life that would enjoy reminiscing."

"Yes. His sister and grandmother." Ginger sounded much relieved. "They live with me, you know. At Hartigan House."

"How lovely."

"Yes," Ginger repeated softly.

"Can you tell me about the gentleman?" Oliver prompted.

Ginger's green eyes glistened. "Perhaps another time. It's rather soon to speak about it."

"Naturally. However, spiritually, you are free to move on, whether it's with this chap or another. The scriptures are clear about this."

For a moment, he'd fancied himself with Ginger Gold. Highly unprofessional, but natural for a single man. At any rate, they'd become friends in the sincerest form, and he had found God's choice for a life mate.

"Oliver?"

Oliver turned to the angelic voice, and the smile lines on his ruddy face deepened.

"Yes, love?"

"What do you think of this dress?" Matilda wore a simple but charming rose-coloured chiffon frock with a large faux flower pinned to the hip. The hem landed modestly at her ankles, revealing T-strapped shoes. "Is it fine?" She spun around to showcase it.

"You're beautiful," Oliver said.

"Thank you, love, but the dress?"

"Oh, yes, it's beautiful too."

Matilda laughed. "I suppose, when you wear the same outfit every day, you don't have to pay attention to fashion."

Oliver laughed with her. He couldn't believe that he'd almost married the wrong girl when, all the while, Matilda was right there under his nose. Not only was she lovely to gaze upon, but she was bright too, a medical student at one time!

His smile faded as Matilda dashed off to the loo and sounds of sickness reached his ears.

"Matilda!"

The toilet rumbled as it was flushed and soon afterwards, his wife reappeared, pale and apologetic.

"Are you ill? Perhaps you should stay behind and rest?"

"I'm fine, Oliver. More than fine." Her hand rested on her abdomen and made slow circles.

Oliver's eyes latched onto Matilda's in question. "You're . . . a b-baby?"

Matilda's face returned to its rosy glow. She nodded with meaning.

Oliver embraced Matilda with raucous enthusiasm and muttered a favourite expression of Ginger Gold's. "Oh, mercy!"

GINGER

Ginger's heart ached for the little boy before her, so clearly in emotional distress. His eyes were reddened with tears; his lower lip quivered. This was her ward, her child, even if society and the law would say it could not be so. Before the lad could answer her, she pulled him to her chest and held him tightly. It was more kindness than the lad could process, and he immediately confessed.

"I did it, missus. I did a terrible fing. I took the master's ring."

His small shoulders shook under the weight of woeful sobs. "I dun't wanna go to gaol. I'll do anyfing if you say I can stay."

"Oh, dear boy," Ginger said. "You're not going to gaol or anywhere but here. Hartigan House is your home and always shall be."

Scout broke away from Ginger's embrace and stared up at her with a look of confusion. "But, missus, I stole from you."

For the second time that day, Ginger produced a handkerchief, though she doubted that would save Scout's sleeve. "Do you have the ring?" she asked.

Scout stuffed a small fist deep into his trouser pockets and with dirty fingers, presented the gold band. He placed it in Ginger's open palm.

"What did you plan on doing with it?"

Scout shrugged. "Nuffink."

"Then why did you take it?"

Scout released a string of short breaths. "If yer din't 'ave the ring, yer couldn't get married to the new master.. Then you'd 'ave more time for me."

Ginger's heart pained deeply. She had been very busy lately, and she had been absent from Scout's daily routine. Lizzie and Mrs. Beasley had readily stepped in, as had Pippins and Clement. Along with the family animals, which Scout adored, Boss and Goldmine, Ginger assumed that Scout was content and happy. It now seemed he needed a mother, a real mother, more urgently than Ginger had thought.

"Oh, Scout. I have been dreadfully busy, but I really should have been more available to you. I promise it shall be different in the future. Even with Mr. Reed living with us. Will you forgive me?"

Scout stared at her, speechless.

"Scout?"

"I should be askin' you, missus, not this other way 'round."

"How about we forgive each other, then?"

"All right." Despite holding her handkerchief, the flannel sleeve continued to do the work.

"Great. Now, we really must both get ready for the wedding. Important duties lie ahead for you and Boss."

A fragile smile. "Yes, missus. I dun't 'ave to 'ave a barf, do I?"

"I don't *h*ave to *have* a bath," Ginger corrected. She reached for the lad's hand. "And yes, I'm afraid you do."

At least there were two mysteries solved. Ginger now knew what had happened to Lizzie and what had happened to Basil's wedding band. Ginger wondered if they would ever discover the real identity of the mystery man who had visited earlier. What did he want if not to steal a ring?

The bouquet of yellow chrysanthemums responsible for her maid's stressful morning sat in a glass vase on Ginger's dressing table. The blooms had perked up during their short time in the water, looking like silk-clad dancers. It really had been a nice idea of Lizzie's, if poorly executed.

Her dress, now removed from its crepe cover, hung elegantly on a clothes hanger that hooked over one of the wardrobe doors.

Lizzie knocked before entering and bent her knees in a slight curtsey. "Are you ready, Lady Gold?

"Yes." Ginger frowned at the time registering on her wristwatch. "I believe I'm destined to be late."

"I'm sure the chief inspector will wait."

"Let's hope so," Ginger said lightly as she removed her dressing gown. Lizzie assisted with the wedding frock, and its silk fabric slipped over Ginger's head like a cold mist of water. It fitted perfectly as Ginger had had it designed and fitted especially for this occasion.

"It's lovely, madam," Lizzie said.

"Yes, but now we must do something with my hair. Have you heated up the curling iron?"

"Yes, madam." Lizzie produced the instrument and

unwrapped it from a protective towel. "It's fresh off the stove."

Ginger seated herself at her dressing table and watched the concentration on Lizzie's thin face as she created shiny, red finger waves. Once Ginger was happy with her hair, she began her makeup. Lizzie was competent enough to apply it for her, but it was something Ginger enjoyed doing herself. Her eyebrows, already plucked in a deep arch, were darkened with a greasy eyebrow pencil. Her eyelids, painted an aqua blue and fringed with two coats of dark mascara, enlarged the appearance of her eyes. She applied rosy spots of rouge under her cheekbones, and peach lipstick warmed her lips.

"You must help me with my veil. Please, be very careful not to let it touch my face." Ginger hadn't time to remove a stain should her makeup brush against it.

Standing in front of her oval floor-length, wood-framed mirror, Ginger gazed at her image. The pearl-grey gown hung from her slender shoulders and tightened about her hips with a matching silk sash attached with a white rhinestone clasp. The netted veil was pinned to her head with a pair of diamond hair clips. Trimmed with delicate white lace, it fell to the floor like a fanciful waterfall.

Lizzie gasped. "You look so beautiful, Lady Gold." Her jaw slackened as she slapped a palm over it. "Oh, dear. I know you shall soon be Mrs. Reed, but I fear, you'll always be Lady Gold to me."

Ginger laughed. "That's quite all right. It takes a while to make a name adjustment, but it happens all the time. You'll get used to it, and you can't go wrong with 'madam'."

Lizzie nodded. "Yes, madam."

BASIL

Basil's fingers deftly tied his black tie and then tucked it into the black waistcoat. His morning coat with tails narrowed slightly at the hips. The trousers were pressed and buttoned up high on his waist. A silk handkerchief was folded neatly in his coat lapel pocket. He nearly used it to wipe his brow but caught himself in time, grabbing a cotton version from the holdall opened on his bed. Sweating? In October? Drat, it must be nerves. Not since the war had he perspired from inactivity. All that waiting in the trenches dodging sniper fire had a way to stoke the adrenaline. Through years of investigating the less-than-honest on the streets of London, he had rarely lost his cool.

Polished leather shoes, a new double-breasted overcoat, and a trilby hat pressed in place, Basil raced down two flights of stairs and out the door—just as a taxicab pulled up in front of Brown's Hotel and a young couple stepped out. Basil's hand shot out to claim it, and he climbed in. Finally, something was going his way.

"St. George's Church," he instructed. "Hurry! I'm late for my wedding."

The cabbie pulled into slow-moving traffic. The driver looked thin in the shoulders, even under a thick autumn coat. His long narrow face needed shaving, and his tired eyes glanced at Basil through the rearview mirror.

"I was married once," he said. "The biggest mistake I ever made. Are you certain the big man upstairs isn't trying to tell ya something?"

Basil scowled. He wasn't about to philosophise about his personal life with a stranger. "I'm certain."

"'Course, I was blinded by beauty. I'm not much to look at now, y' know, but once I was considered a catch by the ladies. Gladys was, one might say, untameable. My mates tried to warn me, but I couldn't 'ear it. I wish to God that I'd listened to 'em."

Basil softened his opinion. He, like the cabbie, had once fallen for a difficult woman whom he could never satisfy. His friends had warned him as well, and Basil had spent many a day and night wishing he'd heeded their warnings.

"Thank you for your concern," Basil said. "But this one is special. I'm a blessed man."

The cabbie nodded his head in solidarity. "I 'ope you're right."

Basil lifted back the cuff of his jacket to check his wristwatch, but his arm was bare. He'd forgotten to put it on.

"Blast it!" He muttered and then froze. Had he forgotten Ginger's ring as well? He dug into his coat pocket and sighed with relief. He removed the small box and stared at the gold band. So small, it barely fitted Basil's little finger. Ginger had such graceful hands with long, delicate fingers. Basil couldn't wait to put it on her. He carefully slipped it back into his pocket.

Basil had never been so fed up with London's growing traffic snarls than he was this instant on Piccadilly. Horses pulled trolleybuses alongside motorcars and buses. Pedestrians took their lives in their hands crossing the busy street wherever they pleased. Basil thought he could walk faster. Suddenly, the taxicab slowed to a stop and reinforced Basil's point.

Basil leaned forward and spoke earnestly. "What's wrong? Why are we stopping?"

The cabbie stretched a long neck out of the window. "Traffic jam ahead. Looks like a lorry tipped its load this side of the Savoy."

Blast it!

Now Basil wished he'd registered at the Savoy Hotel, but Brown's was in Mayfair, close to the townhouse he was vacating, and it had made sense to book a room at the time.

Traffic continued to flow in the other direction. Basil needed to get out and find a taxicab that would take him to the church through an alternate route. He paid the cabbie and got out. As he stood on the side of the road, he watched dusty motorcars and long-suffering horses pulling carts and carriages rumble by, but not a single empty taxicab in sight.

Basil was beginning to think abandoning his taxicab had been a mistake, but he found it had only moved a short distance.

Out of habit, he checked his wrist for the time, only

to find it wasn't there. He didn't even know how late he was. He only hoped that Ginger would wait for him and forgive him. What a rotten way to start their lives together.

"Hey, mate!"

Basil spun on his heel at the sound of a familiar voice. A taxicab had pulled to the kerb and a floppy-haired man with a smile too broad for his face peered out the back window.

"You look like you could use a lift," he called.

"James Smith!" Basil couldn't believe his good fortune.

"Get in old boy," Smith said jovially. "Before the traffic clogs too dearly behind us."

Basil jumped into the back seat of the taxicab before his childhood friend finished his sentence.

"St. George's Church, perhaps?" Smith asked.

Basil grinned, "Pronto!"

Smith leaned in close to the driver as the man inched his way back into the line of motorcars and horses and carts. "You heard the gentleman. Pronto."

With big teeth resting on his lower lip, Smith smiled at Basil.

"You are an angel, my friend," Basil said. "You've saved my life."

"I'd be saving your life if I told our man here to lead us away from the church."

Basil let the comment go. They'd grown up together like brothers, and Emelia, the beautiful siren she had been, had become a wedge between them. It was under-standable that James would be wary. "I see you got my invite. Nice of you to come all this way."

"Ah, it's too hot in Australia anyway. It's their

summer, you know. Imagine Christmas in the blasted heat, not a snowflake in sight. London's been tugging on my heart, dear boy. I miss wearing scarves."

Basil chuckled. "Well, it's good to see you."

"You too," Smith said. "You're a hard man to track down. It helps if you actually put a return address on the envelope."

"I knew I was moving, so I didn't bother."

"Yeah, well, I had to look up the bride, at least you mentioned her in your letter. Went to Hartigan House, but apparently, your girl likes to sleep. The most I could get out of the butler was a suggestion to ring Scotland Yard. At first, I thought he was going to call the coppers on me, but then I remembered you worked there during the war. I admit to being surprised you're still there. You didn't fall into money problems, did you? Because I'd be happy to help you out if you need it." Alarm flashed behind his eyes. "That's not why you're getting married is it? Has Lady Gold got the gold?" He snorted at his pun.

"I don't have financial problems," Basil returned. "I'm not marrying for money. I work because I like my job."

Smith laughed. "You always were the straight one. Anyway, the chaps at the Yard gave me your address in Mayfair, and I was just on my way to find you. Serendipity brought us together!"

It was Basil's turn to laugh. James Smith never had a worry in the world, not growing up and apparently, not now. Even in the war years, he had worked in an office —strings pulled by his influential family—and never saw a weapon fired.

But that was then. Today, Basil was glad to have his

old friend with him on his wedding day. All they had to do was get to the church!

OLIVER

Reverend Oliver Hill wore his usual white robe, but instead of a thick black stole, a gold one hung around his neck. He stood in the doorway of the vestry of St. George's Church. He had a good view of the chancel with its large, newly repaired stained glass window depicting Jesus with his disciples. In the opposite direction were the rows of wooden pews in the nave. Today, the nave was outfitted with white roses and flickering white candles. The small organ on the balcony awaited the organist. The wedding guests awaited the bride and groom.

It was so unusual for both parties to be late. Murmurs of dismay grew louder as each minute ticked by, and Oliver felt compelled to call on the chief organist to head upstairs to the organ loft and play a hymn as they waited. The man was enthusiastic and never played a wrong note, but he lacked emotional dynamic.

At least it wouldn't be a complicated ceremony. Neither Ginger nor Basil wanted a lady or man to stand with them. Basil had mentioned a friend from his youth but hadn't been able to contact him in time.

Oliver adjusted his dog collar. He must remember to instruct Mrs. Davies, the church secretary and parsonage housekeeper, not to use so much starch.

Stepping out of the vestry, he dared a closer look, which caused those in the front to glance up in anticipation. A cursory search confirmed that Ginger's own household had not yet arrived. Oh, dear. He hoped nothing was wrong—that neither the bride nor groom was suffering from, as they say, cold feet.

Matilda caught his eye in question. Oliver smiled, offered a shrug to her and to the others watching him, and stepped back.

He and Matilda had had a rocky beginning, but they were married in the end and now had a little one on the way. Oliver simply couldn't be happier. Undoubtedly, a happy future was also in store for his good friend Ginger Gold.

The front doors of St. George's Church opened followed by a blast of autumn wind and the hurried, flustered rush of persons trying calmly to find their seats. Oliver was relieved to see the Dowager Lady Gold with her granddaughter on her arm. The tapping of her walking stick resounded through the blustering organ music as they made their way to the empty pew at the front. He also recognised the other faces. The maids, Lizzie and Grace, and the tall sour-looking one that the dowager favoured, what was her name? Yes, Langley, and the housekeeper, Mrs. Beasley. With them was Ginger's ward, Scout, who had a leash and Ginger's Boston terrier, Boss. Animals weren't permitted in the sanctuary, but Oliver had made an exception for this occasion.

Leaving her grandmother's side, Felicia Gold headed upstairs and took over the organ duties. The hymn that followed was played delicately, and he could sense the tension in the room lift.

All he needed was the bride and groom to arrive, and he could begin. Suddenly, the door next to the vestry opened.

GINGER

Ginger considered it a sign from above when Basil pulled into the church at the same time she did. Even when late, they were in harmony with each other. She caught his eye and shared a smile. They were both here; they would soon be husband and wife.

Ginger remained in the Crossley with Pippins and Clement, not wanting Basil to see her before she walked down the aisle. Basil tipped his hat and ran down the side of the church in the company of another man.

"I wonder who that is?" she said aloud.

"That's the gentleman who called at Hartigan House this morning," Pippins said. "Mr. Smith."

"Ah. Our mystery man," Ginger said with a smirk. "A friend of Basil's and not a robber after all."

Scout looked uncomfortable in a starched shirt, black bowtie, and the small suit Ginger had specially ordered for him. His face was shiny clean, and his hair washed and slicked back with oil, thanks to Grace who'd stepped in. Beside him, on a white leather leash, sat Boss. He was also newly bathed and brushed. Ginger held in a chuckle. What a pair!

She nodded with a smile, and Pippins ushered Scout and Boss into place behind her. Pausing in the stone archway that opened at the nave, Ginger waited for the first notes of Bach's *Jesu, Joy of Man's Desiring*, and on the cue given by Oliver, Felicia started to play. The melodious tune reverberated off the stone walls, and everyone stood to watch them walk up the aisle.

The church was full, and Ginger registered the familiar faces: her own household, of course, Mrs. Beasley, Lizzie, Grace, Mr. Clement, and Pippins; her staff from her dress shop Feathers & Flair, Madame Roux, Dorothy, and Emma; her neighbour Mrs. Schofield and grandson Alfred; men from Scotland Yard, notably Sergeant Scott and Superintendent Morris. Her friend Matilda, now Mrs. Hill, near the front, across the aisle from Ambrosia.

Ginger captured all these faces in an instant, but her focus was on one man alone, Basil. He stood as if he'd been waiting for her a lifetime. Extraordinarily handsome in his black suit and white shirt, he watched her as if mesmerised; his hazel eyes never left her face. Behind her, she sensed the shy shuffling of Scout, now in lawful possession of Basil's ring, with Boss at his side. Soft murmurs and sniggers reached her ears, and when she got to the front, Ginger turned. She smiled as the small boy and smaller dog settled loudly in their seats beside Sergeant Scott.

Basil reached for her hand and held it gently, yet firmly, in a way that said, I never want to let you go.

A very joyous-looking Reverend Hill stood before

them. When the music stopped, he said, "Dearly beloved, welcome to the marriage of Mr. Basil Reed and Lady Georgia Hartigan Gold." To the couple, he said, "So nice of the two of you to join us." A collective chuckle followed.

He instructed everyone to be seated, then once the noise of the shuffling calmed down, addressed the congregation in a solemn voice.

"We are gathered together here in the sight of God, and in the face of this congregation, to join together this man and this woman in holy Matrimony; which is an honourable estate, instituted of God in the time of man's innocence, signifying unto us the mystical union that is betwixt Christ and his Church; which holy estate Christ adorned and beautified with his presence, and first miracle that he wrought, in Cana of Galilee; and is commended of Saint Paul to be honourable among all men: and therefore is not by any to be enterprised, nor taken in hand, unadvisedly, lightly, or wantonly, to satisfy men's carnal lusts and appetites, like brute beasts that have no understanding; but reverently, discreetly, advisedly, soberly, and in the fear of God; duly considering the causes for which Matrimony was ordained."

The pounding in Ginger's chest made it hard for her to focus on Oliver's words. She thought only of the man who stood before her, the man who loved her, the one whom she loved, and with whom she would spend the rest of her life.

Blackness formed at the corners of her eyes, and her knees grew weak. The great fear she'd kept at bay suddenly attacked: what would she do if Basil died like Daniel had? Could she bear that grief a second time?

"Ginger?"

Basil had her by the elbow; concern etched his brow. He spoke quietly, "Are you all right?"

Ginger blinked, which brought her world back into focus. Oliver's exuberant smile was gone. A silence so quiet filled the church as everyone held their breaths.

Ginger straightened but kept her hold on Basil. "I'm fine. Please continue, Oliver." One must live in the now, Ginger told herself. No one knows the future. One's path must not be dictated by fear but, as Oliver had said so eloquently, by love.

Oliver smiled at the couple before addressing the onlookers. "If anyone can show just cause why they may not be lawfully joined together, let them speak now or forever hold their peace."

Someone cleared her throat after an uncomfortable pause. Ginger's gaze darted towards the sound. Mrs. Schofield! Her small eyes, recessed in a well of wrinkles, sparkled with mischief. Alfred Schofield, her grandson and self-professed lady's man, held back a scoff, and Ginger didn't doubt that the cad would congratulate his mother later. As Ambrosia responded to Mrs. Schofield's minor disruption with a glare, Ginger knew precisely what the Dowager was thinking. Mrs. Schofield wasn't likely to be asked to Hartigan House for tea soon. But then, when had she ever been asked? The sprightly, grandmother always invited herself round.

"It appears there are no objections," Oliver said. He proceeded to lead Basil through the vows and then it was Ginger's turn.

> 'I, Georgia, take thee, Basil
> to be my husband,

to have and to hold
from this day forward;
for better, for worse,
for richer, for poorer,
in sickness and in health,
to love and to cherish,
till death us do part,
according to God's holy law.
In the presence of God, I make this vow.'

Pippins prompted Scout who stepped forward, hands shaking. He handed Ginger the ring. "Thank you," she whispered. He rewarded her with a big toothy smile.

Basil's warm strong hand held hers as he slipped a gold band on her finger and said, "I give you this ring as a sign of our marriage. With my body I honour you, all that I am I give to you, and all that I have I share with you, within the love of God, Father, Son, and Holy Spirit."

Ginger repeated the words to Basil and slid the gold band onto his finger.

The ceremony seemed to pass by in a blur, through the short sermon, and the signing of the register, and before Ginger knew it, Oliver was pronouncing them husband and wife!

Hand in hand, Ginger and Basil strolled down the aisle to the applause and cheers of their friends and family. Outside, Goldmine was waiting in all his glorious glory, adorned in white ribbons and roses and hitched to an ornate black carriage. Clement had arranged for the horse and carriage to be delivered to the church ahead of time, and it was the perfect, magical, ending to a beautiful wedding.

Goldmine, under the direction of a finely dressed Mr. Clement, trotted toward Hartigan House where the reception was to be held.

Basil whispered in her ear. "We did it, Mrs. Reed."

"Yes, we did, Mr. Reed."

Their lips met to the cheers of everyone who watched on as the church bells rang in celebration.

"This is just the beginning of a long, happy, and extraordinary life," Basil said.

Ginger laughed. "I absolutely agree. I can't wait to board the Flying Scotsman and get started on our honeymoon."

Basil patted his waistcoat pocket. "I have the tickets right here."

Ginger wrapped her arms around her groom and kissed him again and Goldmine began the first journey of many they were certain to take together.

I hope you enjoyed *The Wedding of Ginger & Basil.* This book has been edited and proofed, but typos are like little gremlins that like to sneak in when we're not looking. If you spot a typo, please report it to: **admin@laplumepress.com**

Don't miss *Murder Aboard the Flying Scotsman*!

Read on for an excerpt!

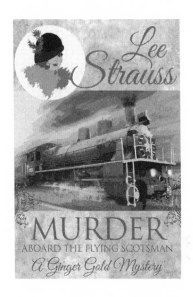

One blustery day in October of 1924, newlyweds Mr. and Mrs. Basil Reed travel aboard the recently christened Flying Scotsman, a high-speed steam engine train that travels from London to Edinburgh, for their honeymoon. With only one short stop at York, Ginger anticipates time with her new husband will fly by.

She's wrong. Something terrible has happened in the Royal Mail carriage which forces the train to stop dead in its tracks. There's been a death and Chief Inspector Reed has been asked to take investigate.

It's a uniquely disturbing murder and Ginger and Basil are eager to puzzle it out together. What do the first class passengers have to do with the dead man? With another crime shortly discovered, Ginger and Basil soon realize they're not dealing with a run-of-the-mill killer—they're dealing with a mastermind who's not done playing with them yet.

AMAZON

Introducing the GINGER GOLD'S BOOK CLUB!

Discuss the books, ask questions, share your opinions.
Fun giveaways! Join the Lee Strauss Readers' Group on
Facebook
for more info.

Love the fashions of the 1920s? Check out Ginger
Gold's Pinterest Board!

Have you joined my Readers Group on Facebook?

fun discussions ○ special giveaways ○ exclusive content

Join my Facebook readers group for fun discussions and first-to-know exclusives!

GINGER GOLD'S JOURNAL

Sign up for Lee's readers list and gain access to Ginger Gold's private Journal. Find out about Ginger's Life before the SS Rosa and how she became the woman she has. This is a fluid document that will cover her romance with her late husband Daniel, her time serving in the British secret service during World War One, and beyond. Includes a recipe for Dark Dutch Chocolate Cake!

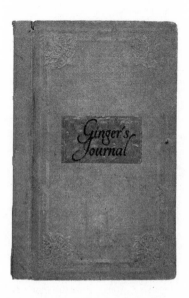

It begins: **July 31, 1912**

How fabulous that I found this Journal today, hidden in the bottom of my wardrobe. Good old Pippins, our English butler in London, gave it to me as a parting gift when Father whisked me away on our American adventure so he could marry Sally. Pips said it was for me to record my new adventures. I'm ashamed I never even penned one word before today. I think I was just too sad.

This old leather-bound journal takes me back to that emotional time. I had shed enough tears to fill the ocean and I remember telling Father dramatically that I was certain to cause flooding to match God's. At eight years old I was well-trained in my biblical studies, though, in retro-spect, I would say that I had probably bordered on heresy with my little tantrum.

The first week of my "adventure" was spent with a tummy ache and a number of embarrassing sessions that involved a bucket and Father holding back my long hair so I wouldn't soil it with vomit.

I certainly felt that I was being punished for some reason. Hartigan House—though large and sometimes lonely—was my home and Pips was my good friend. He often helped me to pass the time with games of I Spy and Xs and Os.

"Very good, Little Miss," he'd say with a twinkle in his blue eyes when I won, which I did often. I suspect now that our good butler wasn't beyond letting me win even when unmerited.

Father had got it into his silly head that I needed a mother, but I think the truth was he wanted a wife. Sally, a woman half my father's age, turned out to be a sufficient wife in the end, but I could never claim her as a mother.

Well, Pips, I'm sure you'd be happy to know that things turned out all right here in America.

Subscribe to read more!

.

ABOUT THE AUTHOR

Lee Strauss is the bestselling author of the Ginger Gold Mystery series and the Higgins & Hawke Mysteries (cozy historical mysteries), a Nursery Rhyme Mystery series (mystery, sci-fi, young adult), the Perception Trilogy (YA dystopian mystery), the Light & Love series (sweet romance) and young adult historical fiction. When she's not writing or reading, she likes to cycle, hike, and kayak. She loves to drink caffè lattes and red wines in exotic places, and eat dark chocolate anywhere.

Lee also writes younger YA fantasy as Elle Lee Strauss.

For more info on books by Lee Strauss and her social media links, visit leestraussbooks.com. To make sure you don't miss the next new release, be sure to sign up for her readers' list!

If you enjoyed reading *The Wedding of Ginger & Basil* , please help others enjoy it too.

Lend it: This ebook is lending-enabled, so please share with a friend.

Recommend it: Help others find the book by recommending it to friends, readers' groups, and discussion boards, and by suggesting it to your local library.

Review it: Please tell other readers why you liked this book by reviewing it on Amazon.

BOOKS BY LEE STRAUSS

On AMAZON

Ginger Gold Mysteries (cozy historical)

*Cozy. Charming. Filled with Bright Young Things. This Jazz
Age murder mystery will entertain and delight you with its
1920s flair and pizzazz!*

Murder on the SS *Rosa*

Murder at Hartigan House

Murder at Bray Manor

Murder at Feathers & Flair

Murder at the Mortuary

Murder at Kensington Gardens

Murder at St. Georges Church

Murder Aboard the Flying Scotsman

Murder at the Boat Club

Murder on Eaton Square

Lady Gold Investigates (short stories)

Volume 1

Higgins & Hawke Mysteries (cozy 1930s historical)

*The 1930s meets Rizzoli & Isles in this friendship depression era cozy
mystery series.*

Death at the Tavern

Death at the Tower

A Nursery Rhyme Suspense (mystery/sci fi)

Marlow finds himself teamed up with intelligent and savvy Sage Farrell, a girl so far out of his league he feels blinded in her presence - literally - damned glasses! Together they work to find the identity of @gingerbreadman. Can they stop the killer before he strikes again?

Gingerbread Man

Life Is but a Dream

Hickory Dickory Dock

Twinkle Little Star

The Perception Trilogy (YA dystopian mystery)

Zoe Vanderveen is a GAP—a genetically altered person. She lives in the security of a walled city on prime water-front property along side other equally beautiful people with extended life spans. Her brother Liam is missing. Noah Brody, a boy on the outside, is the only one who can help ~ but can she trust him?

Perception

Volition

Contrition

Light & Love (sweet romance)

Set in the dazzling charm of Europe, follow Katja, Gabriella, Eva, Anna and Belle as they find strength, hope and love.

Sing me a Love Song

Your Love is Sweet

In Light of Us

Lying in Starlight

Playing with Matches (WW2 history/romance)

A sobering but hopeful journey about how one young Germany boy copes with the war and propaganda. Based on true events.

As Elle Lee Strauss

The Clockwise Collection (YA time travel romance)

Casey Donovan has issues: hair, height and uncontrollable trips to the 19th century! And now this ~ she's accidentally taken Nate Mackenzie, the cutest boy in the school, back in time. Awkward.

Clockwise

Clockwiser

Like Clockwork

Counter Clockwise

Clockwork Crazy

Standalones

Seaweed

Love, Tink

ACKNOWLEDGMENTS

Many thanks go to my editors Angelika Offenwanger, Robbi Brandt and Heather Belleguelle, especially Angelika this time for helping me develop the mystery components!

My assistant Shadi Bleiken who honoured me with an IRL - in real life - wedding by getting married to my son this summer. I couldn't ask for a more kind-hearted and gracious daughter-in-law. She's beautiful inside and out!

So much love to my family, especially my husband, Norm Strauss, for his unwavering faith in me, and to my dear circle: Lori, Donna, Shawn, Norine and Marie.

As always, I'm grateful to my review crew for keeping the reviews coming, and to my Facebook readers' group for reading my books and hanging out with me online. It's so nice to meet up with you there!

The Wedding of Ginger & Basil

A Ginger Gold Mystery companion novella

© 2017 Lee Strauss

ISBN: 978-1-77409-040-4

La Plume Press

3205-415 Commonwealth Road

Kelowna, BC, Canada

V4V 2M4

www.laplumepress.com

Made in the USA
Middletown, DE
28 April 2020

91284498R00061